T0198416

Nana's Thanksgiving Stars?

Sue Gill Harris

WestBow Press books may be ordered through booksellers or by contacting:

WestBow Press
A Division of Thomas Nelson & Zondervan
1663 Liberty Drive
Bloomington, IN 47403
www.westbowpress.com
844-714-3454

Scriptures taken from the Holy Bible, New International Version®, NIV®. Copyright © 1973, 1978, 1984, 2011 by Biblica, Inc.™ Used by permission of Zondervan. All rights reserved worldwide. www.zondervan.com The "NIV" and "New International Version" are trademarks registered in the United States Patent and Trademark Office by Biblica, Inc.®

ISBN: 978-1-6642-7733-5 (sc)
ISBN: 978-1-6642-7734-2 (e)

Library of Congress Control Number: 2022916308

Print information available on the last page.

WestBow Press rev. date: 09/08/2022

WestBow
PRESS®
A DIVISION OF THOMAS NELSON
& ZONDERVAN

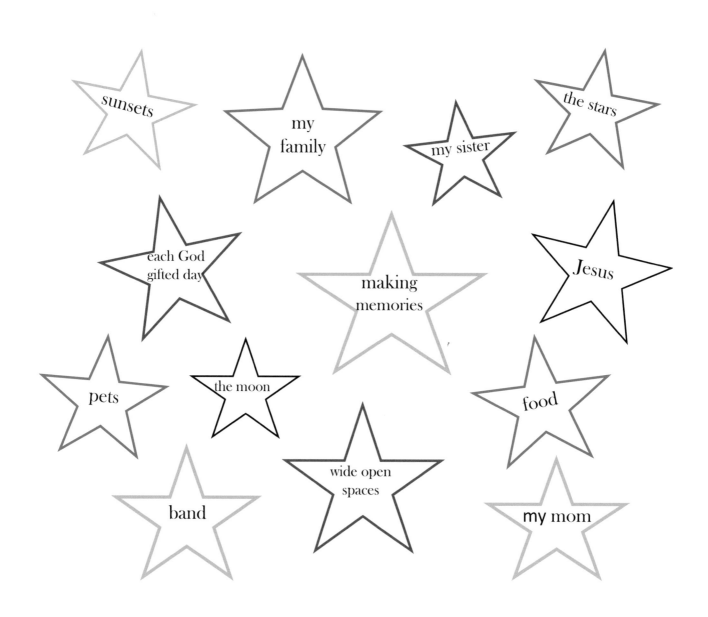

Nana's Thanksgiving

Stars?

In loving memory of my brother,
Larry Ray Gill, who went to be
with the Lord three days after
Thanksgiving 2021
SGH

"I can't believe that **Nana** gave us homework for ***Thanksgiving***!!" Hayley proclaimed from the back seat of the suburban. "We always have fun at Nana's, but getting a homework assignment from your grandmother is weird."

"Well did you do it?" asked her mom from the front.

"I sure did; I don't want to seem ignorant when we talk about stars."

"Stars? What do stars have to do with Thanksgiving?" asked Mom.

"I don't understand it either," said Xander, who was sitting beside Hayley in the back seat. "But I didn't have to study because we did a unit about the Milky Way in science this fall."

School was out for the Thanksgiving holidays, so Xander and Hayley were going to spend "cousins' time" at Nana's, and help her get ready for Thanksgiving. Andi and Rhett, their cousins, were already there when they arrived. When the greetings were done, Nana said, "After dinner tonight, let's watch a Thanksgiving movie, and tomorrow morning we'll make Thanksgiving cookies."

The next morning in Nana's warm, bright kitchen, Nana mixed the dough. As Hayley measured and added the butter, Xander measured and added the sugar, Rhett cracked and added the eggs, and Andi measured and added the flour and spices mixture. Then they rolled the dough on the counter.

As he reached for a cookie cutter, Xander questioned, "why are we making star cookies for Thanksgiving?"

"Because they taste good!" answered Hayley.

"No, I mean how do stars go with Thanksgiving? Why not turkeys or pumpkins?" replied Xander.

"That's what most people would think, but I think stars are a perfect symbol to represent Thanksgiving. Start cutting and I'll tell you why," Nana answered.

As the cousins cut star cookies and placed them on cookie sheets, Nana explained, "Of all the things we should be thankful for, the stars are one of God's **M**ost **M**agnificent **M**arvels!"

"Oh Nana," moaned Xander.

"Well, maybe I did get carried away with my **M**'s, but I love to sit outside on a nice night and gaze at the **m**arvelous stars."

"Were the pilgrims really the first ones to celebrate Thanksgiving?" Hayley inquired.

Rhett replied, "We learned in history that even before the pilgrims came to America, many American Indian tribes had a tradition at harvest time called the 'Green Corn Dance' to show their gratitude to the Creator."

Pans of star cookies now lined the long kitchen counter and Nana said, "I believe we've cut enough stars. Let's add some color to them before we bake them. What colors of sugar sprinkles do we need?" she asked with a wink.

"Is *this* why we had homework?" queried Hayley.

"Partly," Nana answered deviously.

"Oh!" exclaimed Andi, "the Sun is a medium hot star and it's yellow."

"And Betelgeuse, which is red, is one of the coolest stars," inserted Rhett.

"I get it," murmured Hayley, "the very hottest stars are blue or bluish-white."

"So, we need blue, white, yellow, and red sprinkles," stated Xander.

While the cousins cleaned the counter of dough scraps and flour, Nana pulled out red, yellow, white and blue decorating sugar. The cousins then 'colored' the cookies and put batch after batch in the oven to bake as the yummy, sweet smell of baking cookies filled the house.

That evening the moon was bright, as they all sat in the back yard munching on yummy, sweet cookies and looking up at the star-filled sky, Xander pointed up and proclaimed, "look at that bright red star, it's Betelgeuse!"

"Beautiful," whispered Andi.

"Ouuuu," murmured Hayley, as she took a bite of a delicious white cookie, "I see lots and lots of white stars; do you think God made the stars just to make the sky pretty?"

"Oh, no," Andi said, "the stars have been up there helping people for thousands and thousands of years. Do you realize that on the first Thanksgiving the pilgrims and Native Americans probably looked up at the *same* stars we are looking at now?

"Cool, but how do stars *help* people?" Hayley queried.

Rhett jumped in to explain, "Native Americans used the stars, the sun and the moon to tell time, to know the seasons and to know when to plant crops, and early sailors including Columbus and the pilgrims used the stars to guide them across the ocean."

"The stars helped the pilgrims find their way to America!" Hayley exclaimed. "Do you think the pilgrims were ever afraid when they were sailing across the ocean?"

"The pilgrims faced lots of dangers and harsh conditions. Life gets hard for all of us at times; but there is an old song that shows how much God loves us and takes care of us. It's called

Count Your Blessings:

When upon life's billows you are tempest-tossed, when you are discouraged, thinking all is lost, count your many blessings; name them one by one, and it will surprise you what the Lord has done," sang Nana.

"After the pilgrims finally got their homes built, made friends with the Native Americans, who helped them plant gardens and find other food; I'm sure they were thankful for the very same blessings that I thank God for everyday: family, good friends, food to eat, comfortable homes, good health, and safety. Psalm 147:4 says, He determines the number of stars and calls them each by name." quoted Nana. "If He knows the stars so well, just think how well He knows and loves each one of us, His children! And think of all the many blessings he gives us daily."

"What else are you thankful for Nana, and is this more of our homework?" asked Hayley.

With a huge smile Nana replied, "My list is as numerous as the stars, but the list would definitely start with you four! What are each of you thankful for?"

Andi replied, "I'm thankful for my family."

"I'm thankful for Ashley," extolled Rhett.

"I'm thankful for good teachers," stated Xander.

"And I'm thankful my mom helps me with my hair!" praised Hayley

"Okay, you've convinced me, I think stars *are* the perfect symbol for Thanksgiving." Xander admitted.

Nana hugged each grandchild and said, "You better get some sleep; we're making pies tomorrow!"

"Is there homework for that too?" Hayley teased with a cock of her head and a grin.

"*Nighty-night, Nana,*" said Xander with laughter in his voice as they started into the house.

"Nice, Xander!" acclaimed Nana.

"Remember -- count the stars and count your blessings!"

White Sugar Cookies

cup butter, softened
2 cups sugar
4 eggs
4 ¼ cups flour (add another ¼ c if dough is too sticky)
¼ teaspoon cinnamon
⅛ teaspoon nutmeg

Cream butter and sugar. Add eggs, singly, beating well after each addition. Stir flour and spices together. Gradually add to creamed mixture, blending after each addition. Chill. Roll dough, a little at a time, on well-floured surface to 1/8 inch thickness. Cut into desired shapes with cookie cutters. Place on greased baking sheet. Bake 10 – 12 minutes at 350 degrees until lightly browned on bottom. Cookies remain very white. 8 doz.

Thanks to Kay Earnest for the yummy recipe!!

Suggested Activities:

Read the book with your family

Make cookies together

On a clear night, go star gazing like Nana and the Grandchildren did

Look for stars of different colors

Look for particular stars you've read about

Look for constellations

Read: <u>The Pilgrim's First Thanksgiving</u> by Ann McGovern

<u>The First Thanksgiving</u> by Jean Craighead George

Watch: The Mouse on the Mayflower

Sing: Count your blessings

Have a Happy and Blessed Thanksgiving

Enjoy your Family

Count your blessings and thank God for them!

Count Your Blessings.

Rev. J. Oatman. E. O. Excell.

1. When up - on life's bil-lows you are tem-pest-tossed, When you are dis-
2. Are you ev - er burdened with a load of care? Does the cross seem
3. When you look at oth-ers with their lands and gold, Think that Christ has
4. So, a - mid the con-flict, wheth-er great or small, Do not be dis-

cour-aged, thinking all is lost, Count your ma-ny blessings, name them
heav - y you are called to bear? Count your ma-ny blessings, ev - 'ry
promised you His wealth un - told; Count your ma-ny blessings, wealth can
heart-ened, God is o - ver all; Count your ma-ny blessings, an - gels

one by one, And it will sur-prise you what the Lord hath done.
doubt will fly, And you will keep sing-ing as the days go by.
nev - er buy, Your re-ward in heav-en, nor your home on high.
will at - tend, Help and com-fort give you to your journey's end.

Chorus.

Count your bless-ings, name them one by one; Count your
Count your ma-ny bless-ings, name them one by one; Count your ma-ny

bless-ings,see what God hath done! Count your bless-ings,
bless-ings, see what God hath done! Count your ma-ny bless-ings,

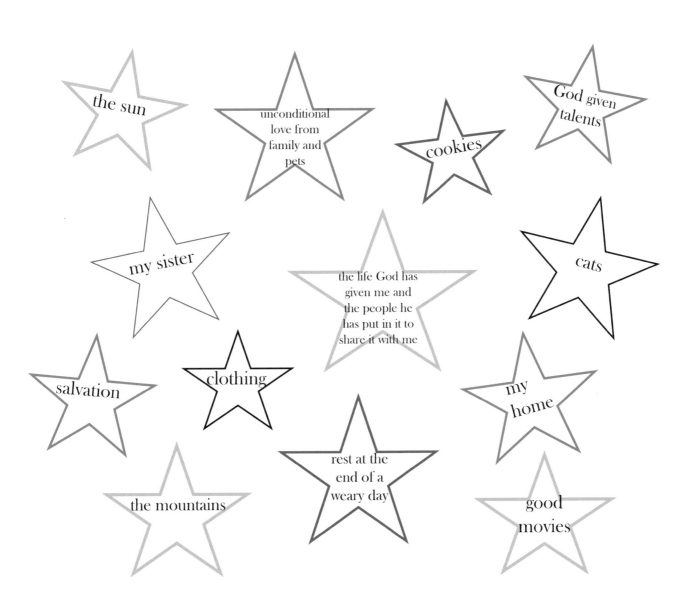

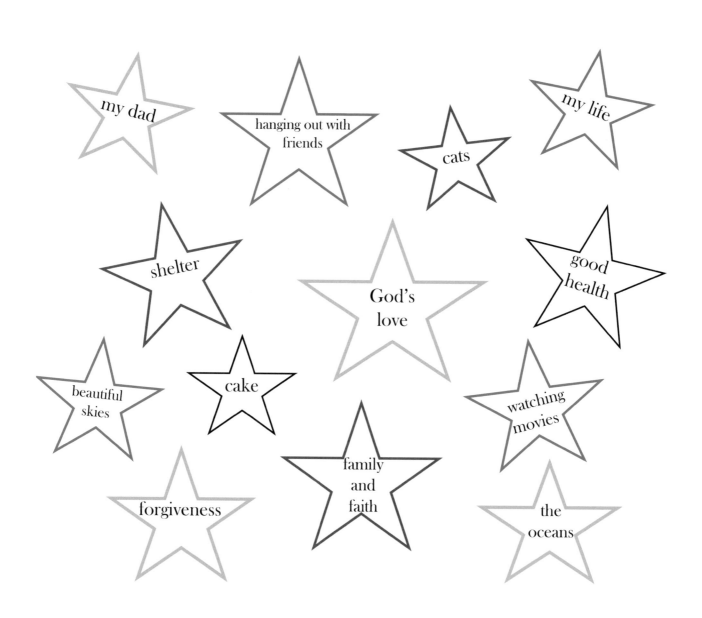

Author Biography

Sue Gill Harris is a child of God, a wife, a mother, a grandmother and a retired (after 42 years) elementary teacher. She enjoys being creative through various hobbies including writing, crocheting, knitting and sewing. Her grandchildren are one of her top priorities. She is also active in her church as a Sunday School teacher and VBS director/teacher.

Printed in the United States
by Baker & Taylor Publisher Services